Our Favorite Day

Joowon Oh

CANDLEWICK PRESS

Every morning, Papa wakes up and drinks some tea.

He waters his plants and tidies up.

Then he gets dressed, puts on his coat, and takes the bus to town.

While he walks through town,

Crafts

Enjoy this Beautiful Day!

he has an idea.

Then he enjoys his favorite lunch—dumplings!

On his way home, Papa notices some flowers growing along the path.

That night, he goes to bed early.

The next morning, Papa wakes up, drinks some tea,
waters the plants, and tidies up.

Then he gets dressed, puts on his coat, and takes the bus to town.

First he stops at the craft store to pick up a few things.

Then he heads to the dumpling house.

On his way home, he stops to pick some flowers.

Then he waits.

I missed you!

Me too!

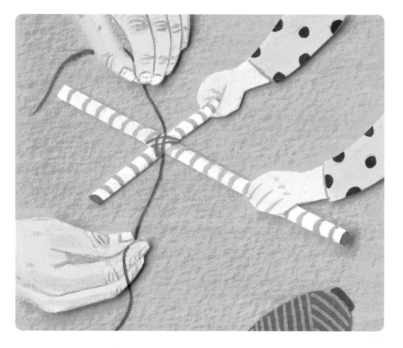

Thursdays are my favorite days.

Mine too.

For my dad, with love

First edition 2019

Library of Congress Catalog Card Number pending
ISBN 978-1-5362-0357-8

19 20 21 22 23 24 CCP 10 9 8 7 6 5 4 3 2 1

Printed in Shenzhen, Guangdong, China

This book was typeset in Sassoon and Hawkins.
The illustrations were done in watercolor, gouache, and cut paper.

Candlewick Press
99 Dover Street
Somerville, Massachusetts 02144

visit us at www.candlewick.com